Visit us on the Web at www.clavisbooks.com.

Just the Right Size written by Bonnie Grubman and illustrated by Suzanne Diederen

ISBN 978-1-60537-365-2 (hardback edition)
ISBN 978-1-60537-428-4 (paperback edition)

This book was printed in June 2018 at Publikum d.o.o., Slavka Rodica 6, Belgrade, Serbia.

First Edition
10 9 8 7 6 5 4 3 2 1

Just the Right Size

Written by Bonnie Grubman
Illustrated by Suzanne Diederen

Clavis

NEW YORK

Did you know . . .
that a *ladybug* is **small** enough
to land on the branch of a tree?

A giraffe is not.

But a *giraffe* is **BIG** enough to reach a treetop without stretching its neck.

A *kitten* is **small** enough
to fall asleep in the flowers.

An ostrich is not.

But an *ostrich* is **BIG** enough
to shade her chicks with her wings.

Did you know . . .
that a *mouse* is **small** enough
to hide almost anywhere?

A moose is not.

But a *moose* is **BIG** enough
to romp in a big pile of snow.

A *goldfish* is **small** enough
to glide through the seaweed.

A dolphin is not.

But a *dolphin* is **BIG** enough
to take you for a swim.

Did you know . . .
that a *hedgehog* is **small** enough
to take a ride on a friend's back?

A giant tortoise is not.

But a *giant tortoise* is **BIG** enough
to be mistaken for a boulder.

A *frog* is **small** enough to perch on a lily pad.

A hippopotamus is not.

But a *hippopotamus* is **BIG** enough to scare even a crocodile away.

Did you know . . .
that a *baby bunny* is **small** enough
to stay dry under a baby elephant?

A mother elephant is not.

But a *mother elephant* is **BIG** enough
to shelter her calf from the rain.

An *ant* is **small** enough
to walk along a blade of grass.

A beaver is not.

But a *beaver* is **BIG** enough to waddle across a log.

DID YOU KNOW . . .
that no matter how **small** or how **BIG**,
you're always just the right size . . .

for a hug!

"I KNOW!"